IRISH FARM ANIMALS

BEX SHERIDAN & GLYN EVANS

ILLUSTRATED BY

BEX SHERIDAN

THE O'BRIEN PRESS
DUBLIN

ABOUT THE AUTHORS

Glyn Evans is a microbiologist with a passion for animal welfare and environmental conservation. Together with his partner and two sons, he lives on a farm in County Meath. It's important to him that his sons grow up with animals around them and can learn about protecting nature. Wanting to share their love of animals with other children and adults, the family opened their farm to the public. Through providing animal therapy, and educating visitors on the small things we can all do to help our environment, they hoped to reduce animal cruelty. While the farm is no longer open to the public, Glyn continues to reach out to both children and adults and help them to understand the importance of animals and the environment. Find out more at his Facebook page, 'Trim Alpacas'.

Glyn (and alpaca)

Bex Sheridan is an artist, writer and graphic designer with a great love of animals. She is often asked to illustrate animals, from pet portraits to wildlife. As a child, Bex dreamed of having a house filled with animals when she grew up – which is what she now has! She and her husband Jay have their own mini-menagerie: it began with one rabbit and now there are also dogs, birds (of many kinds), a lizard and even a hedgehog! As a child, however, Bex thought farms were boring (yes, despite the love of animals). It wasn't until visiting Glyn's farm that she discovered how farm animals are no different from the pets we know and love!

Bex (and quail)

DEDICATION

To Jay and Jen, our partners in crime

ACKNOWLEDGEMENTS

We would like to thank Pat Divney, Thomas Reaney, Joseph Lawrence, Johnny Lynch, Brenda Boyne, Jack Dixon, Arthur Preston, Adeola Thompson, our wonderful editors Nicola Reddy and Emer Ryan, and everyone at the O'Brien Press, for their knowledge and contribution.

Published in:

DUBLIN
UNESCO
City of Literature

First Published 2020 by The O'Brien Press Ltd,
12 Terenure Road East, Rathgar, Dublin 6, D06 HD27, Ireland.
Tel: +353 1 4923333; Fax:+353 1 4922777
E-mail: books@obrien.ie
Website: www.obrien.ie
The O'Brien Press is a member of Publishing Ireland.

Copyright for text, illustrations and design © Bex Sheridan 2020
Copyright for editing © The O'Brien Press Ltd

ISBN 978-1-78849-121-1

Photographs by Bex Sheridan; Johnny Lynch (buffalo, p. 13); Shutterstock (pigs, p. 16; ponies, p. 30); Jack Dixon (donkey, p. 32).

7 6 5 4 3 2 1
23 22 21 20

Printed and bound in Drukarnia Skleniarz, Poland.
The paper used in this book is produced using pulp from managed forests.

CONTENTS

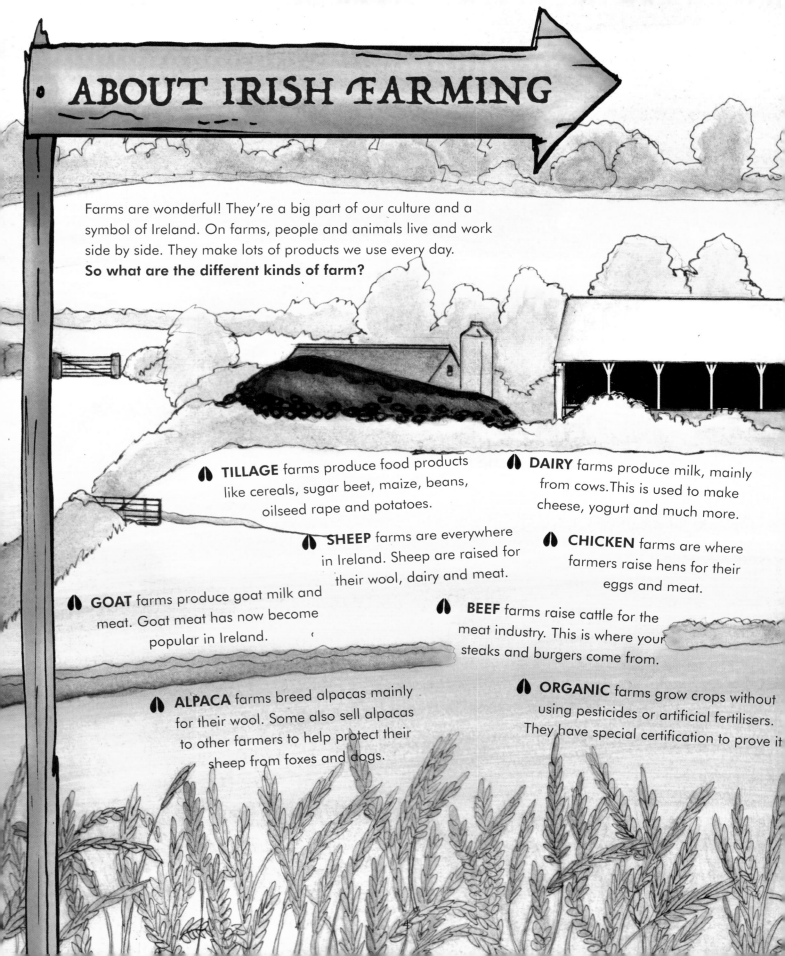

ABOUT IRISH FARMING

Farms are wonderful! They're a big part of our culture and a symbol of Ireland. On farms, people and animals live and work side by side. They make lots of products we use every day.
So what are the different kinds of farm?

TILLAGE farms produce food products like cereals, sugar beet, maize, beans, oilseed rape and potatoes.

DAIRY farms produce milk, mainly from cows. This is used to make cheese, yogurt and much more.

SHEEP farms are everywhere in Ireland. Sheep are raised for their wool, dairy and meat.

CHICKEN farms are where farmers raise hens for their eggs and meat.

GOAT farms produce goat milk and meat. Goat meat has now become popular in Ireland.

BEEF farms raise cattle for the meat industry. This is where your steaks and burgers come from.

ALPACA farms breed alpacas mainly for their wool. Some also sell alpacas to other farmers to help protect their sheep from foxes and dogs.

ORGANIC farms grow crops without using pesticides or artificial fertilisers. They have special certification to prove it.

And of course, there are **PET** farms. These are where you come to see the animals up close, and you sometimes get to touch them! A zoo inspector visits a pet farm to make sure the animals are healthy, with houses, enough space and plenty of food and water.

FARMING ...

... began in Ireland around 4000BC, during the New Stone Age. Farmers made and used some of the first-ever tools! By 1845, two-thirds of Irish people relied on the land for their food. Today, though the number of farms is going down, their size is going up. Look out for farm events like the National Ploughing Championships, farmers' markets and animal shows all around Ireland!

FARMING SEASONS

The four seasons are very important in farming, for many reasons. Certain things need to happen at certain times.

SPRING

March - April - May
Everything, from plants to animals, is waking up after winter. The farmer is preparing for new arrivals. All the farm animals that spent winter indoors are let back out onto pastures. Some farmers keep pregnant animals in the sheds until they have had their babies. This means the farmer can keep an eye on them.

During spring, the plant life starts to come back. Grass starts to grow and leaves start to appear. Unfortunately for the farmer, so do the weeds. Keeping weeds down throughout spring and summer can be a full-time job for organic farmers. Non-organic farmers spray a chemical on them to kill them. This is the easiest option but is bad for the rest of nature.

Bees are important on farms because they pollinate many plants that people and animals eat. Many crop and fruit farmers in Ireland keep or rent beehives for their farms.

Follow the bees through spring and summer to see where they've been.

SUMMER

June - July - August
This is when we see some sun, or so we hope! The heat and the longer days are good for the babies who were born in spring. They put on weight faster and grow stronger. This will make them ready for winter.

Farmers repair sheds and fences that may have been damaged during the winter months.

Summer is the time of year when farmers make hay or silage. They will feed these to the animals inside throughout the winter.

WINTER

December - January - February
The animals are brought into sheds and fed inside. All the food has to come in too. It's a big job for farmers.

It can be hard for farmers, with the cold and wet weather. Moving around can be difficult if it gets very muddy.

Egg farmers get fewer eggs from chickens as it becomes dark.

The animals need fresh straw to sleep on. The straw must be changed every few days. Some farmers try to keep their animals outside for as long as possible but it depends on the weather.

Watch out for the snowflakes! Whenever you see these, it means the animals need to go into bed in a shed when winter comes.

AUTUMN

September - October - November
This is when the leaves fall from their trees. The crop farmers are preparing to harvest their crops. The crops will then be sold to large factories. The factories clean and sell on the crops to be made into other products.

The animals born in spring are big and strong now. Most of them will be sold for meat. Some will be kept to use for breeding.

The farmers might get a second cut of hay or silage in autumn but it won't be as much as in the summer.

OUR HORNED HEROES

COWS

So what was on these farms more than 4,000 years ago? Cows!

Cows were currency: a person's wealth was measured by the number of cattle they owned. But of course cows are much more than that.

They are individuals with unique personalities. Some have a favourite feeding trough, some have a favourite place to lie down … and some even like to play football! And they're all very curious. If something new enters their field, they go straight over to investigate.

Cows are '**ruminant**' with a multi-chambered stomach. This means that they have lots of parts to their stomachs: four, in fact! Humans are monogastric, so we have only one stomach.

LIKES AND DISLIKES

- Cows love the sun. They graze grass early in the morning to late in the evening, so that they can spend the best bits of a sunny day lying down, enjoying the heat. Normally they eat all day long.

- They love a good swim but they hate puddles; they're afraid of their own reflection!

- They hate stony ground.

- They don't like loud noises or strangers. Always be gentle when approaching a cow field.

The world's oldest cow was called Big Bertha. She was a Droimeann cow from Sneem, Co Kerry. She died in 1993 at the age of 48.

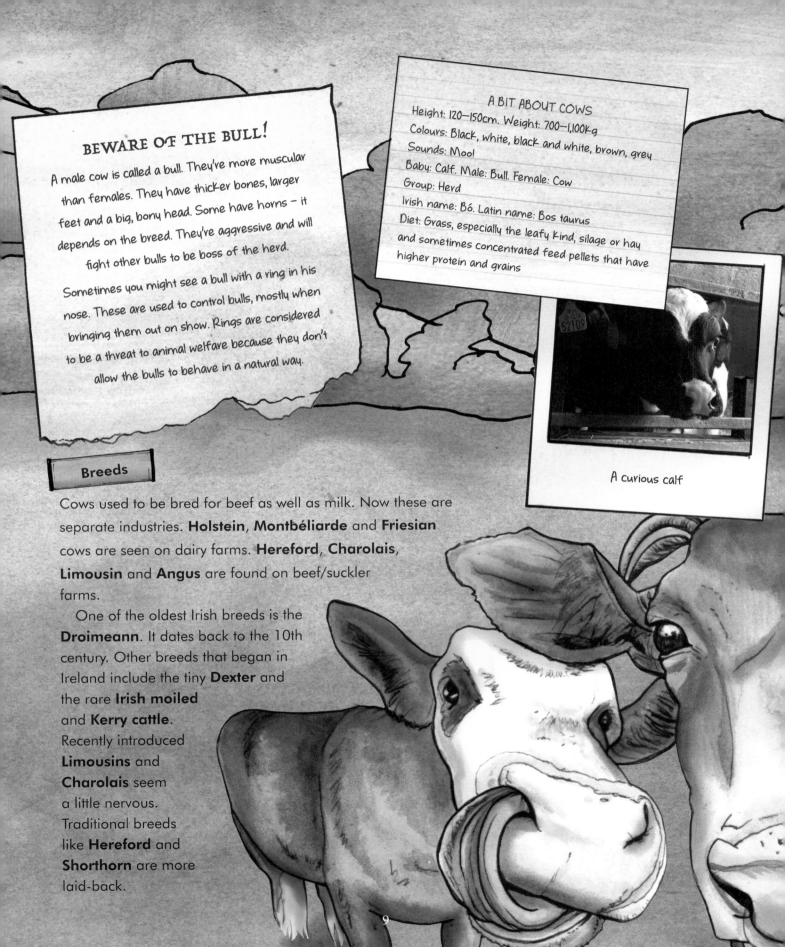

BEWARE OF THE BULL!

A male cow is called a bull. They're more muscular than females. They have thicker bones, larger feet and a big, bony head. Some have horns – it depends on the breed. They're aggressive and will fight other bulls to be boss of the herd.

Sometimes you might see a bull with a ring in his nose. These are used to control bulls, mostly when bringing them out on show. Rings are considered to be a threat to animal welfare because they don't allow the bulls to behave in a natural way.

A BIT ABOUT COWS

Height: 120–150cm. Weight: 700–1,100kg
Colours: Black, white, black and white, brown, grey
Sounds: Moo!
Baby: Calf. Male: Bull. Female: Cow
Group: Herd
Irish name: Bó. Latin name: Bos taurus
Diet: Grass, especially the leafy kind, silage or hay and sometimes concentrated feed pellets that have higher protein and grains

A curious calf

Breeds

Cows used to be bred for beef as well as milk. Now these are separate industries. **Holstein**, **Montbéliarde** and **Friesian** cows are seen on dairy farms. **Hereford**, **Charolais**, **Limousin** and **Angus** are found on beef/suckler farms.

One of the oldest Irish breeds is the **Droimeann**. It dates back to the 10th century. Other breeds that began in Ireland include the tiny **Dexter** and the rare **Irish moiled** and **Kerry cattle**. Recently introduced **Limousins** and **Charolais** seem a little nervous. Traditional breeds like **Hereford** and **Shorthorn** are more laid-back.

GOATS

Goats are full of character – mostly a mischievous character, but that's what makes them so entertaining!

They'll eat anything, even the washing on your clothesline or the aerial on your car. They love to play and jump and they are great escape artists, so farmers need to put very good fencing around their goat fields. However, they do hate the cold and really, really, hate the rain, so they must have shelter available to them at all times.

Farmers like goats because:
- They're fun to have around!
- They are great weeders and hedge-cutters. Goats can clear hilly land so quickly they prevent wildfires.
- They are a source of meat and milk.

Old Irish Goats

In 2018, two rare 'geeps' were born in Co. Mayo. They may be the world's only surviving twin sheep/goat hybrids!

A BIT ABOUT GOATS

Height: 40–60cm. Weight: 20–140kg

Colours: Light to dark brown and with white, brown or black markings, as well as white, grey or black

Sounds: Bleat!

Baby: Kid. Male: Buck or billy. Female: Doe or nanny

Group: Tribe or trip

Irish name: Gabhar

Latin name: Capra aegagrus hircus

Diet: Plants, trees, weeds, hay and grains

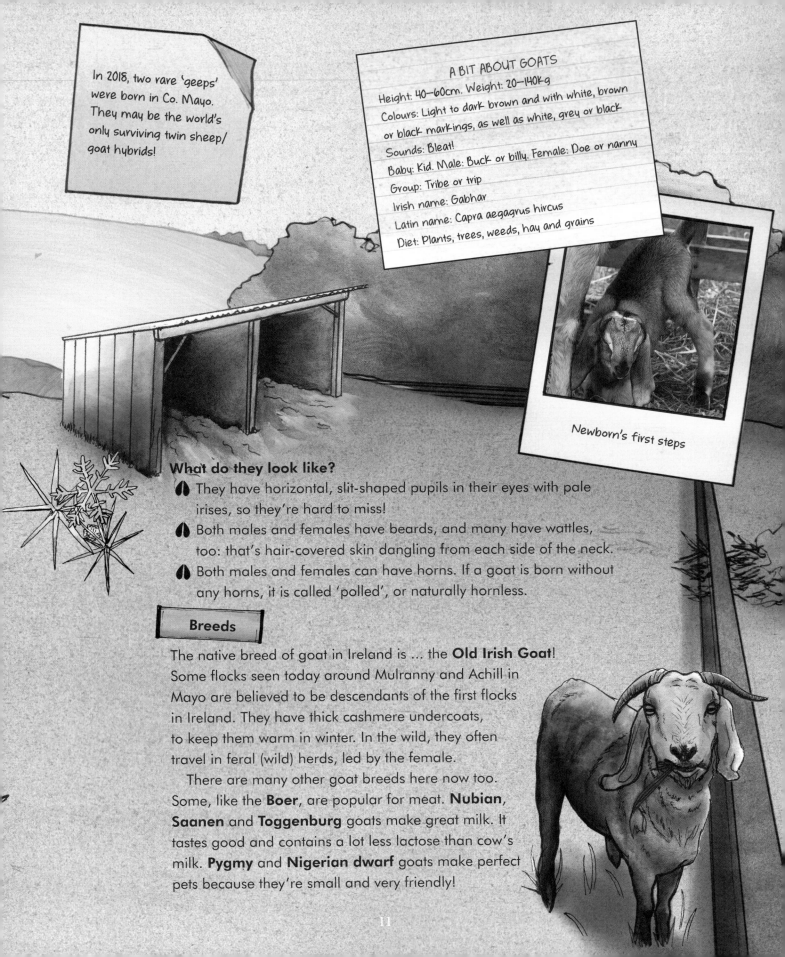

Newborn's first steps

What do they look like?

- They have horizontal, slit-shaped pupils in their eyes with pale irises, so they're hard to miss!
- Both males and females have beards, and many have wattles, too: that's hair-covered skin dangling from each side of the neck.
- Both males and females can have horns. If a goat is born without any horns, it is called 'polled', or naturally hornless.

Breeds

The native breed of goat in Ireland is ... the **Old Irish Goat**! Some flocks seen today around Mulranny and Achill in Mayo are believed to be descendants of the first flocks in Ireland. They have thick cashmere undercoats, to keep them warm in winter. In the wild, they often travel in feral (wild) herds, led by the female.

There are many other goat breeds here now too. Some, like the **Boer**, are popular for meat. **Nubian**, **Saanen** and **Toggenburg** goats make great milk. It tastes good and contains a lot less lactose than cow's milk. **Pygmy** and **Nigerian dwarf** goats make perfect pets because they're small and very friendly!

BUFFALO

Buffalo can be very friendly – a domestic buffalo is more like a dog than a cow!

Buffalo live all over the world. Some are called water buffalo. These first came to Ireland in 2009. The first herd was brought from Italy by Johnny Lynch from County Cork. He now has over two hundred buffalo. He runs the popular Macroom Buffalo Cheese company. There are other buffalo keepers in Ireland now too, and many more to come!

12% of the world's milk comes from buffalo.

What buffalo like

- They like to know what's going on. Some buffalo are nosy and love opening gates.
- In Asia, where water buffalo come from, they like to graze in swamp land. Here in Ireland they enjoy a good wallow in the mud and scratching against trees.
- They like rain and damp weather. They don't like sunny weather. This makes Ireland ideal.

BUFFALO VS BISON

Buffalo are not to be confused with bison, which also belong to the Bovidae family. From time to time, you can visit bison in Tayto Park, County Meath.

🐾 **Bison** have a much bigger head than **buffalo**. This makes them better battering rams!

🐾 **Bison** horns are like cow horns. **Buffalo** horns are bigger with sweeping arcs.

🐾 **Bison** have a hump and a beard. **Buffalo** don't.

🐾 **Bison** are from North America. **Water buffalo** are Asian. **Cape buffalo** are African.

A BIT ABOUT BUFFALO

Height: 2.5m (head & body)

Weight: 680–1,200kg

Colours: Black, grey, brown

Sounds: Grunts, mumbles and even gargles!

Baby: Calf. Male: Bull. Female: Cow

Group: Herd

Irish name: Buabhall

Latin name: Bubalus bubalis

Diet: Grass, haylage, herbs and plants

Happy Cork buffalo

Buffalo are large and look a lot like cows, but their bodies and horns are a different shape. Buffalo horns stretch almost five feet and they have deep ridges on the surface. Both males and females have horns, though the females have smaller ones.

Buffalo milk is richer in fat and protein than cow's milk. There is less fat in buffalo meat than there is in beef. It tastes different too!

DAIRY

Dairy refers to any food made from the milk products of animals.

Computer monitoring milking

A bit about dairy

- Most dairy comes from cows but some comes from goats, sheep and buffalo too.
- Animals are raised and milked on dairy farms and the milk is prepared for use in dairy products.
- Dairy contains lots of nutrients: a glass of milk has calcium, protein, iodine, potassium, phosphorus and vitamins B2 and B12. These are all very important for our bodies' growth and health.
- Cows start to produce milk just before they give birth to a calf. The calf drinks the mother's milk to get big and strong.
- Once the calf is eating solid food, it leaves its mother and the mother is milked for another few months.

- Cows produce milk for up to ten months. They produce most milk in the forty to sixty days after the birth of the calf.
- Eating grass gives cows around 20 litres of milk per day; if they eat extra hay, haylage or concentrated cow feed, they can produce more milk.
- In the old days, cows were milked by hand. Today, farmers have milking machines to help them.

Milking machines

These machines are big and look scary, but the cow's comfort and safety are important. Cows are good at taking their turn – maybe this is because they get their dinner while being milked! A computer monitors each cow by name to make sure that she is not distressed.

What happens next?

The milk is stored in stainless-steel, chilled tanks until the creamery lorry comes to collect it. At the creamery, it's put into cartons for drinking or made into dairy products like butter, cheese, yogurt and ice-cream.

Inside a modern milking machine

Old-fashioned milking parlour

At Dublin Zoo's Family Farm, you can learn how to milk a cow and make butter from scratch! You can also visit a milking jersey herd at Airfield Estate in Dundrum in Dublin.

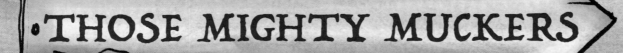

THOSE MIGHTY MUCKERS
PIGS

Pigs are fun and friendly. They love to eat and play with toys. They enjoy a good belly-rub, just like a dog!

Pigs love to roll in the mud. This helps them to keep cool in summer and stops annoying flies from landing on them. They like tasty bugs. Their dished faces make it easy to dig up mud to find them! A grassy lawn won't last long around a pig. They hate being cold and wet though. A nice warm, dry house is a must. They don't like being alone, they are social animals, so they should always have a friend for company!

A BIT ABOUT PIGS
Height: 50–100cm. Weight: 50–350kg
Colours: Pink, red, brown, black, white
Sounds: Oink! Grunt!
Baby: Piglet. Male: Boar. Female: Sow
Group: Litter
Irish name: Muc.
Latin name: Sus scrofa domesticus
Diet: Grass, bugs, worms, grubs, roots, nuts, fruit, as well as food and grains from farmer

Two pigs talking

PIG ARKS

A pig house is called an ark, and it usually looks like a tunnel. It's made from curved sheets of metal over a wooden frame with a door on one end. It can be made from plastic, too.

To keep pigs, even as pets, you need to be a registered pig keeper. Everything you need to know is online at the National Pig Identification & Tracing System (NPITS).

Breeds

The common pink pig that we know and love is a British breed called the **Landrace Large White cross.** They are raised for pork. When **Landrace** and **Large White** were bred together, the result was a pig that produced more meat than either breed on its own. They have pointy ears, slightly dished faces, long bodies and fine white hair. And they are very large!

Some farmers raise **rare-breed pigs** for their personalities, rarity and meat, which has a different flavour. They are super hardy and perfect to raise outdoors, free-ranging. Rare breeds usually need the vet less often than pink factory pigs, as they spend so much time outside in the air.

On the following pages, we'll meet three rare-breed pigs found in Ireland: the **Wild boar**, the **Iron Age pig**, and the **Kunekune**.

Pigs talk to each other constantly. Newborn piglets know their mother's voice. Many can recognise their own name by two weeks old! Sows even 'sing' to their young whilst nursing.

RARE-BREED PIGS

Wild boar feeding time

WILD BOAR

Wild boar are the ancestors of most pigs. They used to roam the forests of Ireland but became extinct here centuries ago. Now they are found only on farms.

They have a different nature from common pigs. Their meat also tastes different. Their bristles can be used to make hair and beard brushes!

WARNING!

Never get close! They can be aggressive. In the UK, a farmer must have a Dangerous Wild Animal licence to keep them. It's not as strict in Ireland, but it's still important to be careful around them.

A BIT ABOUT WILD BOAR
Height: 55–120cm. Weight: 60–100kg
Colours: Brown, red, black, grey
Irish name: Torc fiáin
Latin name: Sus scrofa
Diet: Grass, bugs, worms, grubs, roots, nuts, fruit, as well as food and grains from farmer

A pair of nosy kunekune

A BIT ABOUT IRON AGE PIGS

Height: 70–100cm. Weight: 120–160kg

Colours: Red, black, brown, stripy

Irish name: Muc Iarannaois

Diet: Grass, bugs, worms, grubs, roots, nuts, fruit, as well as food and grains from farmer

Newborn Iron Age piglets

IRON AGE PIGS

Iron Age pigs are a cross between **wild boar** and another very old breed called **Tamworth**. They are friendly like the **Tamworth** but strong-willed like **wild boar**. They are hardy so are happy to live outside. They look like pigs from ancient times, which we see in Iron Age drawings. **Tamworth** are descended from the **Irish Grazier**. They are super energetic and love to run and play. **Iron Age pigs** like to run and play too.

A BIT ABOUT KUNEKUNE

Height: 60cm. Weight: 60–200kg

Colours: Black, brown, blond, ginger and white or a combination of all

Diet: Grass, nuts, fruit, as well as food and grains from farmer in the winter months

KUNEKUNE

The **kunekune** is the ideal pet pig. They are smaller than other pigs – though they still grow quite big! Their name, pronounced 'cooney cooney', means 'round and fat'. They don't need loads of food and easily make friends with people, pets and other livestock. They don't dig like other pigs, because they have smaller noses – they prefer to graze grass and even live happily in a household garden (so long as they have some shelter).

ROTAVATING

Rotavating means breaking up the surface of the ground by digging and turning soil.

REASONS TO ROTAVATE

- Preparing a seedbed for plants to grow

- Weed control

- Preventing the soil from getting clogged. Without rotavation, the top of the ground dries and cracks, and water runs right through, drowning the plant roots.

- Aeration. This means putting small holes in the soil to allow air, water and nutrients to reach the roots. When the roots absorb these, they grow deeper and stronger!

NATURE AT WORK

Pigs are nature's rotavators, thanks to the wonderful plough on the end of their noses! As a pig digs the land, he goes to the toilet on it too. This makes the soil fertile and ideal for growing next year's vegetables.

SOWING SEEDS

Some farmers prepare and plan to sow their crops in spring. They want the plants to get as much light as possible from the summer sun.

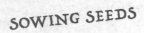

Wild boar rotavating

Wild boar are very energetic and love to dig, making them great rotavators.

AUTUMN HARVEST

The crop farmers are preparing to harvest their crops. The crops will then be sold to large factories. The factories clean and sell on the crops to be made into other products.

Many different farm implements are used to till the land and make it ready for planting. A rotavator (or cultivator) is used to do this over large spaces of land. It's a big machine that needs lots of fuel and maintenance.

THE WOOLLY ONES

SHEEP

Sheep enjoy company and have best friends – this could be another sheep, a goat or even a person!

Sheep are quiet, gentle and obedient. In their flocks they have a leader who they respect.

Different breeds of sheep look a little different from one another, but most have wool. Some have hair, though. These 'hair sheep' don't need to be sheared.

Sheep's wool, or fleece, is the most popular animal fibre in the world. It is used to make clothing and other materials.

Farmers keep sheep for their meat and milk too.

A BIT ABOUT SHEEP

Height: 85–140 cm

Weight: 45–160kg

Colours: White, black, brown

Sounds: Bleat, baa!

Baby: Lamb, lambkin, cosset

Male: Ram. Female: Ewe

Group: Drove, flock, herd or mob

Irish name: Caora. Latin Name: Ovis aries

Diet: Grass, pasture plants and sheep meal

LAMBING

When sheep are born, it's known as 'lambing' and this is an important part of spring for farmers.

Sheep know what plants to eat as medicine when they've sick.

There are approximately 4.8 million people and 3.73 million sheep in Ireland. That's almost as many sheep as people! Every December, the Department of Agriculture conducts a National Sheep and Goat Census to keep track!

A friendly Suffolk sheep

Breeds

There are many breeds of sheep in Ireland. **Blackface mountain sheep** are the most common on upland farms. They include types from Mayo/Connemara, Kerry, Waterford and Donegal. They're super hardy, so they can survive the cold, wind and rain. This makes them perfect for our upland farms.

The most popular breed on lowland farms is the **Suffolk**. They're fatter with great woolly fleeces, and they grow really fast. The first flock in Ireland was registered by Henry Strevins from Roscommon in 1891. They have spread quickly since.

Blackface Mountain Sheep

ALPACAS

Alpacas are very calming animals, with unique personalities. This makes them wonderful to have around!

They are sweet and gentle, and seem timid. But they are kept on farms to protect sheep from predators – they'll happily chase away a fox or dog! They're generally very friendly but they don't like being petted on the head. They love a good roll in the dust, though!

A BIT ABOUT ALPACAS
Height: 80–100cm. Weight: 50–85kg

Colours: Most commonly brown, white, black and fawn

Sounds: Humming

Baby: Cria. Male & female: Alpaca

Group: Herd

Latin name: Vicugna pacos

Diet: Grass, alfalfa hay, sheep nuts, flaked maize, rolled barley, special alpaca food and monthly vitamins A, D and E

Alpacas strike a pose

Alpacas arrived in Ireland in 2001, but people in Peru kept them 6,000 years ago. In their native Peru, they are used for hiking and carrying materials.

The Inca people of Peru valued them most for their wool, which they called 'The Fibre of the Gods'. Alpaca wool is still prized today: it's hypoallergenic and used for clothing, insulation, duvet and pillow stuffing, felted hats and even for removing dead skin.

ALPACA VS LLAMAS

Alpacas are often mistaken for llamas. Both are species of Camelid. If you see a 'llama' in Ireland, it's more likely to be an alpaca! Alpacas and llamas can mate with each other; the baby is known as a Huarizo.

Llama wool is not as valuable because it's much coarser.

Alpacas' ears are straight. **Llamas'** ears look more like bananas.

Be careful not to get on their bad side! Like camels, alpaca like to spit and they can kick like a horse too.

Alpacas are the friendlier of the two.

Llamas are bigger than **alpacas**.

LIFE IN IRELAND

Alpacas spend their farm life in herds. If they are privately owned, they are always kept in at least pairs. They can live on all kinds of bumpy terrain, as long as they have grass to graze and some shelter. They don't mind extreme temperatures but prefer the cold. All of this makes them perfect for Ireland!

Alpacas always poop in the same spot and their poop is high in nutrients so it's great for plants!

WOOL

Wool is like a coat for some animals: it keeps them warm in cold weather and dry in wet weather.

When we have our coats on during the summer, we get too hot, so we take them off. It's the same for sheep, llamas, alpacas and some goats.

When the weather gets warmer, around May in Ireland, their wool needs to be sheared. If it isn't, they could overheat, which is very dangerous. Sheep don't like being sheared, but they're happy once it's done! Over the following months, they grow their wool back and have nice coats again by winter.

DIFFERENT KINDS OF WOOL

- **Lambswool** comes from a first shearing. Before the sheep is seven months old, its wool is at its softest.

- **Merino wool** is the softest and finest sheep wool. It is named after the Merino breed.

- **Cashmere** comes from the undercoat of Cashmere goats. It is like Merino wool.

- **Angora** wool is plucked from Angora rabbits. It's very soft but not very ethical.

- **Mohair** is a frizzy wool from the Angora goat.

- **Alpaca wool** is like sheep wool but softer, finer and naturally hypoallergenic.

- **Llama wool** is weaker and coarser than alpaca wool, and rarer too.

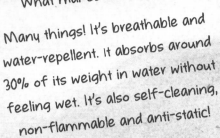

What makes wool great?

Many things! It's breathable and water-repellent. It absorbs around 30% of its weight in water without feeling wet. It's also self-cleaning, non-flammable and anti-static!

An alpaca being sheared

26

Shearing is done by professionals using a shear.
The shear is like a hair clippers but more powerful, with
a bigger blade. It's usually electric. There are also hand-held
shears that look like scissors. These are harder to use and shearing
with them takes longer, so the sheep gets more stressed. After
shearing, the fleece is cleaned in a factory and spun into balls of
wool. These are brought to a woollen mill and made into clothes.
Wool can also be used as insulation to keep our houses warm.

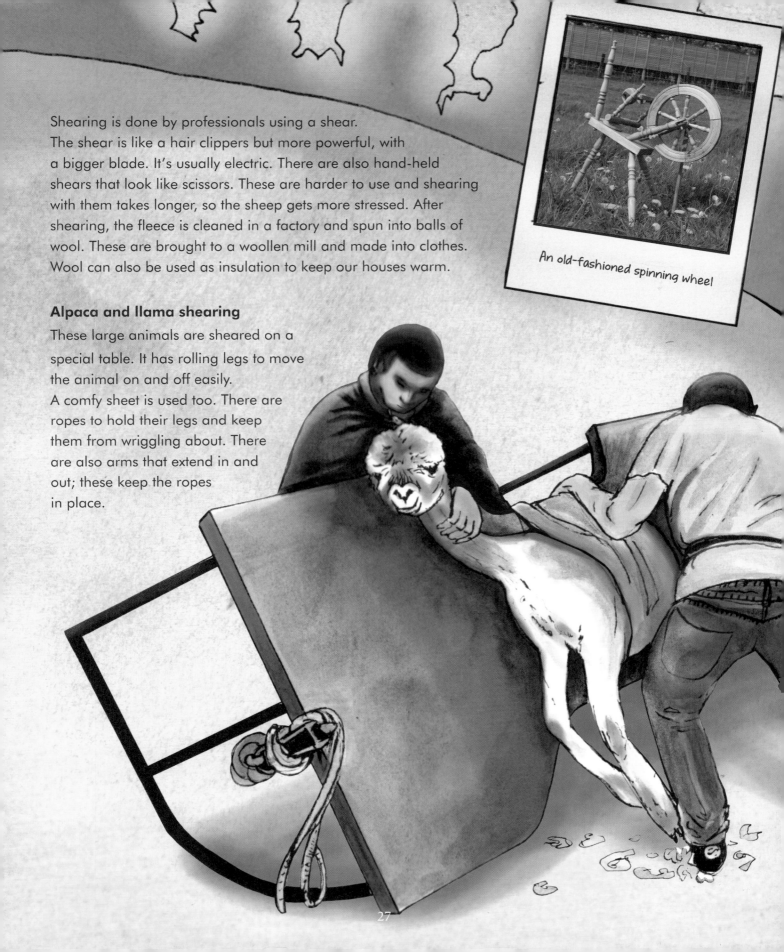

An old-fashioned spinning wheel

Alpaca and llama shearing

These large animals are sheared on a
special table. It has rolling legs to move
the animal on and off easily.
A comfy sheet is used too. There are
ropes to hold their legs and keep
them from wriggling about. There
are also arms that extend in and
out; these keep the ropes
in place.

THESE HOOFED HECKLERS

HORSES

Horses love to learn, especially tricks like bowing and lying down. They learn troublesome tricks too, like how to escape their stables and raid the haybarn!

Horses are real individuals. Some are bold and brave leaders. Others are timid and happy to follow. Some are cheeky and enjoy making mischief. All are super smart. They use their ears and body language to communicate.

In the days before machinery, every farm had to have horses. They pulled ploughs through fields and helped farmers to transport goods. These days, they are mostly kept for breeding, racing and equestrian sports. They have long legs and big bodies, making them strong and fast – they can run within hours of being born! Their faces and necks are big and long too, and they love being rubbed near their neck, on their withers.

Stables

Horses are kept in stables. Stables offer protection from bad weather, a place to chat to other horses and somewhere to grab a dry bite to eat. Stables must be big enough to walk around in and sturdy enough to take a kick! Claustrophobia and boredom cause stress, though, so it's important that stables have windows.

Breeds

Ireland is famous for its horse breeders, trainers and jockeys. Many breeds we see today are descended from the **Irish Hobby**, an ancient and now extinct breed. It was fast and light, used for racing and in battle. The popular **Irish Draught** is one of its descendants. Another popular breed is the stout, powerful **Irish Cob**.

Ready for riding

Horses are measured in hands.
1 hand = 10cm or 4 inches.

FACES
A horse can have different markings on its face. Horses have the largest eyes of any land animal!

blaze
stripe
bald
star
snip

Despite their strength and size, horses really dislike flies. They can feel a teeny tiny fly land on their backs. They use their tails, which are made of hair, to swish flies away. They have hair on their heads and necks, too. Horsehair is used to make violin bows, paintbrushes, fabrics, jewellery, pottery and fishing line.

A BIT ABOUT HORSES
Height: 140–180cm. Weight: 380–1,000kg
Colours: Brown, black, chestnut, grey, white
Sounds: Neigh, whinny or bay!
Baby: Foal. Male: Stallion. Female: Mare
Group: Harras
Irish name: Capall
Latin name: Equus caballus
Diet: Hay, alfalfa, grass, pellets of concentrated feed

PONIES

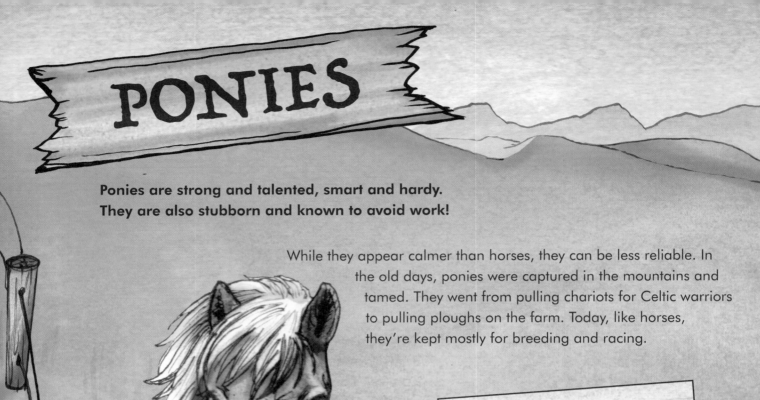

**Ponies are strong and talented, smart and hardy.
They are also stubborn and known to avoid work!**

While they appear calmer than horses, they can be less reliable. In the old days, ponies were captured in the mountains and tamed. They went from pulling chariots for Celtic warriors to pulling ploughs on the farm. Today, like horses, they're kept mostly for breeding and racing.

A BIT ABOUT PONIES
Height: 110cm–144cm. Weight: 200–350kg
Colours: Mainly chestnut, brown, black, grey, white
Sounds: Neigh, whinny or bay
Baby: Foal. Male: Stallion. Female: Mare
Group: Harras
Irish name: Capaillín
Latin name: Burdo
Diet: Grass and pony nuts (but not racehorse cubes!)

A pair of Connemara ponies

Breeds

The hardy, athletic and friendly **Connemara pony** comes from the west of Ireland. Some people believe that they were bred from ponies brought to Ireland by the Vikings. The Viking ponies may have been bred with the **Irish hobby**. Other people say that they were bred from Spanish Armada horses that swam ashore from a shipwreck. The Connemara Pony Breeders' Society holds an annual Connemara Pony Show, where people can see ponies from all around the world.

Another old Irish breed is the **Kerry bog pony**, which is calm, strong and lovely for farm and family. At one point, it almost became extinct. There was only one remaining male, called Flashy Fox. He became father to many more, and now the **Kerry bog pony** is officially recognised as a pedigree pony.

In 1963, Dr Fred Wilshire became the first person to import a Connemara pony to Australia. It was called Island King. Now Connemara ponies are popular in Australia!

HORSES VS PONIES

The main difference between the two is height. But there is a little more to it than that!

- **Ponies** are less than 14.2 hands (144cm). **Horses** will always be bigger.

- **Ponies** are better in colder weather than **horses**.

- **Ponies** have different bone structure, muscles and body proportions.

- **Ponies** are stockier and stronger for their size.

- **Ponies** are more stubborn!

DONKEYS

Donkeys love to shout, but that's not always a bad thing – it just means that they're really happy to see you!

Donkeys are sweet and friendly, smart and gentle. But sometimes they shout when they're unhappy. They hate being alone, as they're very social animals. They will bond with a companion for life.

Donkeys have a long history in Ireland, even though they're not native. Our donkeys are probably descended from the **Nubian wild ass** and the **Somali wild ass**, both from Africa. They began cross-breeding on their journey along the Silk Road, while transporting silk and spices.

How are donkeys different?
- They look quite like horses but are smaller, usually somewhere between the size of a horse and a pony.
- Their ears are longer than horses' ears and their manes are stiff and upright,.
- Their tails look very different, with short hair until the end, which has a brush of longer hair.

A BIT ABOUT DONKEYS
Height: 79–160cm. Weight: 80–480kg
Colours: Grey, brown, black, brown-and-white or black-and-white markings; rarely white
Sounds: Braying or hee-haw!
Baby: Foal. Male: Jack. Female: Jenny, jennet
Group: Drove, pace, herd
Irish name: Asal. Latin Name: Equus asinus
Diet: Grass, barley straw, hay, sugar beets and vegetables as treats

Donkey looking for carrots

Donkeys, like horses and ponies, only bed down for winter if it's a really bad one. Normally they are given jackets to keep them warm.

Donkeys were once used on farms for clearing stones from fields, grinding corn, moving turf from bogs, and transporting manure, potatoes, milk and other produce. They even did the dangerous job of moving seaweed, sand and shells. They transported the family and were beloved pets. As times changed, they became popular as riding animals.

Donkeys are also kept on farms with no other livestock, to keep the field grass short.

Unless you're experienced, it's tricky to train a donkey. They can be stubborn, but with care and patience they can learn lots.

A mule is a cross between a male donkey and a female horse. The less-common cross between a female donkey and a male horse is called a hinny.

TRANSPORT

Horses, ponies and donkeys were the original tractors for farmers!

They used to pull the plough to sow seeds, and the cart to take the grains, meat and milk to market. They also transported the farmer and his family. They lost these jobs around the 1940s, as tractors became more popular. However, as fuel and maintaining machinery get more expensive, some farmers are working with these wonderful animals again!

In the 1800s, many people couldn't afford to keep horses. Donkeys became known as 'the poor man's tractor'. In the rocky west of Ireland, carts weren't always suitable for transportation – but the sure-footed donkey was!

Donkeys had baskets called panniers attached to them, and sometimes a special type of sled, known as a slipe, that could be used to help them to transport things.

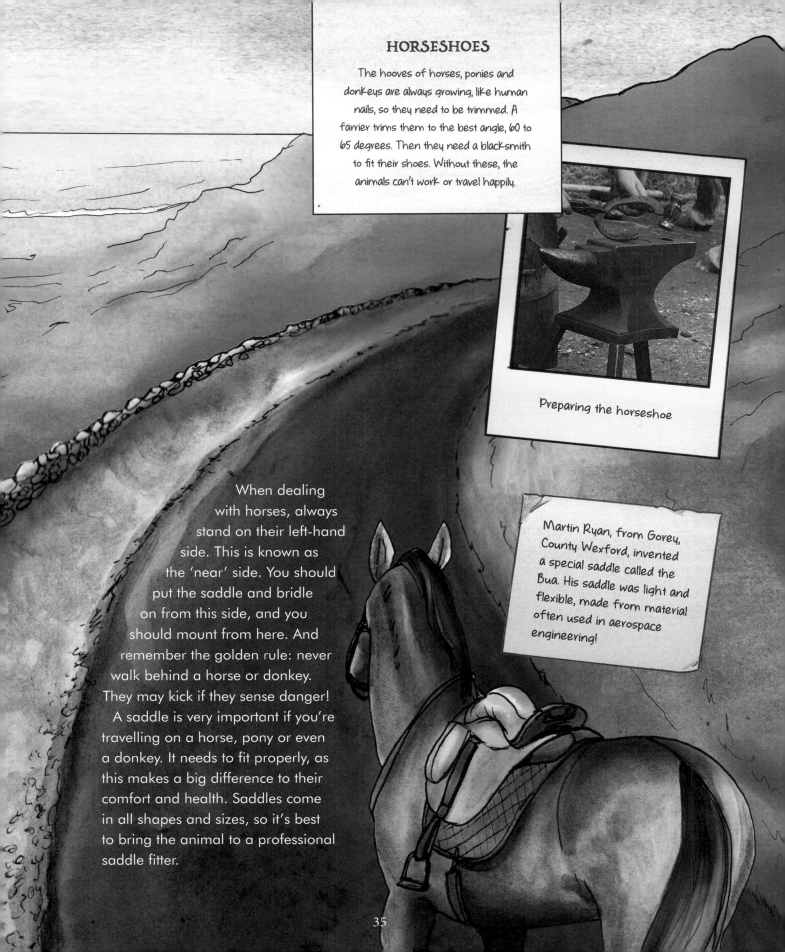

HORSESHOES

The hooves of horses, ponies and donkeys are always growing, like human nails, so they need to be trimmed. A farrier trims them to the best angle, 60 to 65 degrees. Then they need a blacksmith to fit their shoes. Without these, the animals can't work or travel happily.

Preparing the horseshoe

When dealing with horses, always stand on their left-hand side. This is known as the 'near' side. You should put the saddle and bridle on from this side, and you should mount from here. And remember the golden rule: never walk behind a horse or donkey. They may kick if they sense danger! A saddle is very important if you're travelling on a horse, pony or even a donkey. It needs to fit properly, as this makes a big difference to their comfort and health. Saddles come in all shapes and sizes, so it's best to bring the animal to a professional saddle fitter.

Martin Ryan, from Gorey, County Wexford, invented a special saddle called the Bua. His saddle was light and flexible, made from material often used in aerospace engineering!

OUR FEATHERED FRIENDS

CHICKENS

Chickens are friendly birds that give you a present every morning for your breakfast!

Chickens are kept on farms to produce eggs and catch insects. They keep giving eggs if they are happy – and they are happy if they are loved, have lots of space, and are fed nice food and given plenty of water. Chickens are also sometimes kept for meat.

THE CHICKEN COOP

Chickens have their own kind of house, called a coop. The ideal minimum for one chicken is 2,800–3,800cm² (3–4 square feet) of coop space. If they spend more time in their coop, they should have at least 9,300cm² (10 square feet). It needs to be in a place that gets lots of sun, a nice breeze and is easy to access.

Corrugated or felt roof to keep water out

Windows/ventilation, for light and air

Nesting box, to lay in

Feeder and waterer

Run for being outdoors

Perch area inside top — they love sleeping on perches

Poop boards below the perches for easy cleaning

A chicken tractor is a temporary coop where they can stay safe, go on adventures, and also trim the grass for you and deal with pesky insects. It has wheels and handles and can be moved easily.

A busy rooster

A BIT ABOUT CHICKENS

Height: 40–60cm. Weight: 600g–4.5kg

Colours: Brown, black, white and many mixtures

Sounds: Chickens cluck, chicks chirp, cocks squawk, and hens crow!

Baby: Chicks and biddies or broilers when bred for meat

Male: Cockerel (under 1 year of age) and cock (over 1) in the UK and Ireland; rooster in the US, Canada, Australia and New Zealand. Female: Pullet (under 1 year of age) and hen (over 1)

· Group Name: Brood or flock

Irish name: Cearc

Latin name: Gallus gallus domesticus

Diet: Pellets that help them to lay more eggs, grains, vegetables, meal worms, insects, slugs, snails

Chickens have a fleshy part on top of their heads. It is called a comb, or cockscomb. They also have hanging skin under the beak, called wattles; together, these are called caruncles! Like other birds, chickens have wings, but they can't really fly. However, some breeds (the lighter ones) can get quite far over fences and into trees.

Chickens have been in Ireland for a long time, but they didn't become popular here until the 14th century. They were kept more for their eggs than their meat.

Traditionally, chickens roamed the fields during the day and were brought into the warm kitchen at night.

There are many types of chicken in Ireland. Some large breeds have a bantam, or miniature, version. These are small and friendly and are often kept as pets.

QUAIL

A BIT ABOUT QUAIL

Height: 18–22cm. Weight: 90–130g

Colours: White, brown, blonde, striped, spotted, patched

Sounds: Chirp, cheep, beep and ca-caw!

Baby: Chick. Male: Cock. Female: Hen

Group: Flock, covey, or bevy

Irish name: Gearg

Latin name: Coturnix coturnix

Diet: Chicken pellets, seeds, cereals, insects and vegetables

Quail are little round birds that make great pets. They all have their own funny personalities.

Quail are often calm, easy to hold, and will follow you around. The chicks are often striped and so small when they hatch that they can look like bumblebees! They live happily indoors, where they become good friends with their humans. They also live outdoors in a coop, like chickens. They prefer to live in pairs or small groups. In big groups, they will fight.

Quail out exploring

They're kept mostly for their eggs. Quail eggs are more nutritious than chicken eggs. They contain good cholesterol and lots of vitamins A, B1 and B2. They also contain a protein which can help with allergies. They are sometimes kept for their meat, too.

In the wild, **common quail**, or **European quail**, live mostly in bushes and tall grass. They're migratory birds but they prefer not to fly. They are rare in Ireland but nests have been seen in Galway, Mayo, Offaly and Kildare. It's hard to spot them, though, since they're excellent little hiders.

They make a funny noise known as the 'wet my lips' call. This is often the only way you'll know they're around!

The domestic quail you see on farms are actually **Japanese quail**, or a cross between **European** and **Japanese quail**.

A quail protects itself by freezing. If that doesn't work, it will jump really high out of danger's reach.

MALE QUAIL

Male quail strut. They walk around with their necks pushed straight out, parallel to the ground. They make a loud crowing noise when looking for friends.

Ducks have great personalities! They live in Ireland both in the wild and on farms.

Ducks are kept on farms for their big, tasty eggs. Sometimes they're raised for meat. Duck meat is fattier but tastier than chicken.

Ducks are also handy to have around to eat pests like snails and slugs. Some snails carry a parasite called liver fluke. This is very bad for many animals – but not for ducks!

Breeds

Ducks come in lots of shapes and colours, but they all start out as fluffy bundles of joy. Different breeds will mix on the farm, but a bigger one might bully a smaller one, so sometimes it's safer to separate them. Most are descended from the wild **mallard**; the only breed that isn't is the **Muscovy** duck, originally from Mexico, Central and South America. The Muscovy duck likes to roost in trees.

WATERFOWL

Ducks, geese and swans are known as waterfowl. They all have webbed feet and flattened bills. Their feathers have an oily coating. This makes them excellent at shedding water.

Ducks like to have a pond to play in. Unlike most animals, they love the rain! They don't like direct sunlight, so they need shade in the summertime.

A BIT ABOUT DUCKS

Height: 50–75cm. Weight: 1.3kg–2.4kg
Colours: Most commonly white, brown, black and green
Sounds: Quack!
Baby: Duckling. Male: Drake. Female: Hen
Group: Flock
Irish name: Lacha
Latin name: Anas platyrhynchos
Diet: Small fish, fish eggs, snails, worms, slugs, and on the farm they eat water fowl pellets

GEESE

There's nothing cuter than a gosling. And there's nothing scarier than a fully grown goose!

On the farm, geese enjoy free-ranging on grass; they keep it from getting too long. They like to have shelter, but it takes really bad weather to convince them to use it. While geese are waterfowl, they don't need a large pond of water – but they certainly enjoy having one.

Farmers keep geese for a few reasons:

- They make great guards! They're big and loud and not afraid to chase down danger.
- They lay enormous eggs that taste much like chicken eggs.
- They're raised for meat too. Goose is very popular for Christmas dinner.

Geese were domesticated over 4,000 years ago in Egypt. In Ireland, you'll see both wild and domestic geese. Domestic geese can't fly. Wild white-fronted geese can fly, though. They come here every winter from the Arctic tundra parts of Europe, Siberia and Alaska. There aren't as many winter visitors as there used to be, though, because they like boggy land, and bogland in Ireland is under threat.

A week-old gosling

A BIT ABOUT GEESE

Height: 75cm–115cm. Weight: 3kg–6.5kg

Colours: Most commonly white, grey, black and brown

Sounds: Honk!

Baby: Gosling. Male: Gander. Female: Goose

Group: Gaggle

Irish name: Gé. Latin name: Anserinae

Diet: Grass, grains and waterfowl pellets and layers' pellets when they're laying eggs

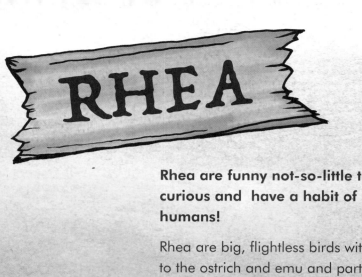

RHEA

Rhea are funny not-so-little troublemakers. They are very curious and have a habit of pecking buttons and stealing from humans!

Rhea are big, flightless birds with long legs and necks. They are related to the ostrich and emu and part of the ratite family, which means that they can't fly. Although they can appear a little timid, they get along with many other farm animals.

They live on grassland, grazing happily. They need a shed for shelter and a decent amount of land on which to stretch their long legs. A good fence will keep them from going on adventures.

A BIT ABOUT RHEA

Height: 90–110cm to their back.

Weight: Up to 40kg

Colours: Grey, white

Sounds: Mostly silent but during mating season, they make a booming noise!

Baby: Chick. Group: Flock

Latin name: Rhea americana

Diet: Plants, fruit, seeds, small animals like frogs and lizards, small birds

Rhea dads dig the nests and sit on the eggs until they hatch. They also raise the babies until they wean.

Father and chick

Rhea naturally prey on rodents, frogs and insects – helping to keep the farm rodent-free. They are known as omnivores; this means they eat both meat and plants.

The rhea on farms in Ireland are usually the **greater rhea**, also called **common rhea**. Another kind of rhea is the **lesser rhea**, also called **Darwin's rhea**, which are a little smaller. Both are originally from South America. They were first imported to Ireland from the UK. They're gradually spreading across Europe, though – wild **greater rhea** have even been spotted around Germany!

RHEA VS OSTRICHES VS EMU

Rhea are from South America, **ostriches** from South Africa and **emu** from Australia.

Rhea have blue to brown eyes. **Emu** have orange eyes. **Ostriches** have brown eyes.

Rhea and **emu** have three toes on each foot. **Ostriches** have only two.

Rhea are the smallest. **Ostriches** are the largest birds in the world.

Rhea are the easiest to keep fenced in.

EGGS

Just hatched, inside incubator

Eggs come in all sizes and colours, but they are all a similar shape.

Eggs have a tapered end (they get gradually narrower). This makes them less likely to roll out of the nest. They also have strong shells so they won't break when the mother sits on them.

Some birds have white eggs, some blue or green. Mature emu eggs look black. Eggs can have spots, sometimes so many that they look like one colour. A free-ranging chicken will have different shell colours from one that lives inside. The yolk colour can be different, too, depending on diet.

Egg size depends on the bird that lays it; a quail lays tiny eggs, but an ostrich lays huge ones.

CANDLING EGGS

Candling means holding a torch (or candle) to an egg in the dark to see through its shell. The first signs of life can be seen around day 10, when the chick looks like a little spider. These are its veins. An air bubble forms when the chick is getting closer to hatching. Sometimes you can even see them move inside the egg!

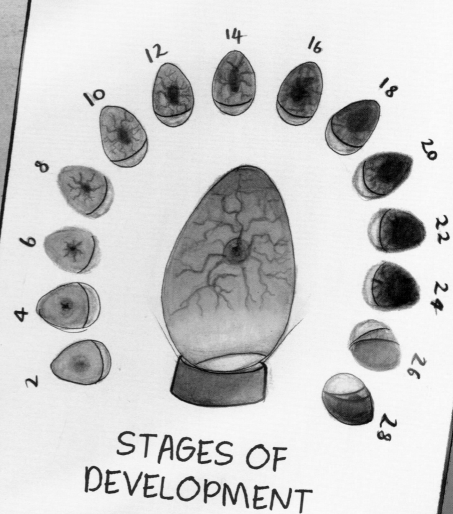

STAGES OF DEVELOPMENT

When a chicken wants to have babies, she lays her eggs in a nest. She sits on them to keep them warm. She also turns them many times a day. This allows the baby chick to grow properly in its shell. Around day 21, the baby starts to peck the shell from inside and cracks a hole in it. This is called 'pipping'. Then they turn around in the shell which is called 'zipping'. Finally they crack the shell down in a line, 'unzipping' it, and slowly climb out.

The mother keeps the babies warm until they're ready to leave the nest. When they're big enough, the mother takes her babies outside. She teaches them how to find food and have fun. After 6 to 8 weeks, the chicks leave their mother to continue their own adventure!

INCUBATION TIMES FOR DIFFERENT BIRDS

Bird	Incubation (days)	Turning
Most Poultry	21	19
Cotunix Quail	16–18	14
Turkeys	28	26
Ducks	28	26
Muscovy	35–37	34
Geese	28–30	27
Rhea	35–40	34
Ostrich	42	40
Emu	50–56	49

INCUBATION

Sometimes birds aren't very good at hatching their own eggs, especially when they're young or the weather is bad. The farmer can help out by putting the eggs into an incubator. Like a mother hen, an incubator keeps the eggs warm and humid and turns them many times a day until close to hatching time.

When they hatch, the chicks are left in the incubator until they're dry and fluffy (about 8 to 12 hours). Then they're moved to a box called a brooder. They're kept warm in the brooder with a heat lamp and are fed by the farmer.

For 6 to 8 weeks, the farmer cares for them. The temperature is reduced by 5 degrees every week, until the babies are strong enough to go outside and enjoy the sunshine with their friends.

Laying
Chickens and many other birds lay more eggs as the days get longer.

THE HAPPY HELPERS

DOGS

The trusty sheepdog is an important animal on the farm!

Sheepdogs help farmers to round up sheep and other animals. They even round up chickens and ducks. Sheepdogs are trained well and trusted greatly. They have a strong bond with the farmer, as both spend a lot of time together.

Breeds

The word sheepdog might make you think of a black-and-white **border collie**. But many breeds are used as farm dogs. The best for herding and guarding are larger breeds, which have loud barks, train well and enjoy helping out.

Some breeds that are thought of as dangerous or scary, such as **German shepherds**, are actually fantastic farm dogs. The **Himalayan sheepdog**, with its thick, warm coat, can even sleep in the field with the sheep. **Terriers** help farmers by catching mice and rats that steal food and spread sickness.

CATS

The need for farm cats may be the reason why they were domesticated to begin with!

Since around 7500 BC, cats have helped by catching mice and rats. Rodents are a big problem around the farm. They chew holes in food bags and eat what's inside. They also pee on things, spreading disease.

Some people believe that farm cats won't catch pests if they are well fed. This is not true – they need proper meals of cat food too. Being healthy and happy helps them to do a better job.

46

FROGS & HEDGEHOGS

Some wild animals are very helpful on Irish farms.

If farmers are growing vegetables, they might find that snails and slugs come out at night-time to eat them all. Luckily, frogs and hedgehogs come out at night to look for food, too. They will eat as many bugs as they find!

The farmer can help these little creatures by building houses for them. Frogs will move into a small pond that's not touched by other animals. Little shelters will attract hedgehogs.

WINTER TIME

When winter comes, some of the outdoor animals are brought inside.

HEDGE TRIMMING

Hedges are cut in late autumn/early winter. In Ireland, there is a law against cutting hedges between 1 March and 31 August. This is to protect the wildlife.

The animals need to be fed a couple of times a day. So, during the summer, farmers start making hay or silage or growing grains to feed them. They also keep the straw to make comfortable beds for them.

The farmer has to put out bedding many times a week to keep the animals dry and warm. At the end of winter, all the manure has to be cleaned out of the shed.

It would be easier for the farmer if the animals were out eating grass all year, but during Irish winters this is not always possible!

Farm machinery must be washed, serviced and stored during the winter, too. This keeps it in good condition for the following year.

Even with the year at its end and the animals tucked up inside, there is still so much to do. But in the end it's all worth it to be a part of the wonderful world of farming.